GOSCINNY AND UDERZO

PRESENT

An Asterix Adventure

ASTERIX
AND THE
MAGIC CARPET

Written and Illustrated by ALBERT UDERZO

Translated by ANTHEA BELL *and* DEREK HOCKRIDGE

© 1987 GOSCINNY/UDERZO

Original title: *Astérix chez Rahāzade*

Exclusive licensee: Orion Publishing Group
Translators: Anthea Bell and Derek Hockridge
Typography: Bryony Newhouse

This revised edition first published in 2002 by Orion Books Ltd,
Orion House, 5 Upper Saint Martin's Lane, London WC2H 9EA

5 7 9 10 8 6 4

Printed in France by Partenaires

http://gb.asterix.com
www.orionbooks.co.uk

A CIP record for this book is available from the British Library

ISBN-13 978 0 75284 715 3 (cased)
ISBN-10 0 75284 715 5 (cased)
ISBN-13 978 0 75284 776 4 (paperback)
ISBN-10 0 75284 776 7 (paperback)

Distributed in the United States of America by Sterling Publishing Co. Inc.
387 Park Avenue South, New York, NY 10016

BELGICA

GAULISH VILLAGE

COMPENDIUM

LAUDANUM

AQUARIUM

TOTORUM

ARMORICA

LUTETIA

SPQR

GAUL
(ROMAN CONQUEST)
50 BC

CELTICA

AQUITANIA

PROVINCIA

THE YEAR IS 50 BC. GAUL IS ENTIRELY OCCUPIED BY THE
ROMANS. WELL, NOT ENTIRELY . . . ONE SMALL VILLAGE OF
THE INDOMITABLE GAULS STILL HOLDS OUT AGAINST THE
INVADERS. AND LIFE IS NOT EASY FOR THE ROMAN LEGION-
ARIES WHO GARRISON THE FORTIFIED CAMPS OF TOTORUM,
AQUARIUM, LAUDANUM AND COMPENDIUM . . .

ASTERIX, THE HERO OF THESE ADVENTURES. A SHREWD, CUNNING LITTLE WARRIOR, ALL PERILOUS MISSIONS ARE IMMEDIATELY ENTRUSTED TO HIM. ASTERIX GETS HIS SUPERHUMAN STRENGTH FROM THE MAGIC POTION BREWED BY THE DRUID GETAFIX . . .

OBELIX, ASTERIX'S INSEPARABLE FRIEND. A MENHIR DELIVERY-MAN BY TRADE, ADDICTED TO WILD BOAR. OBELIX IS ALWAYS READY TO DROP EVERYTHING AND GO OFF ON A NEW ADVENTURE WITH ASTERIX – SO LONG AS THERE'S WILD BOAR TO EAT, AND PLENTY OF FIGHTING. HIS CONSTANT COMPANION IS DOGMATIX, THE ONLY KNOWN CANINE ECOLOGIST, WHO HOWLS WITH DESPAIR WHEN A TREE IS CUT DOWN.

GETAFIX, THE VENERABLE VILLAGE DRUID, GATHERS MISTLETOE AND BREWS MAGIC POTIONS. HIS SPECIALITY IS THE POTION WHICH GIVES THE DRINKER SUPERHUMAN STRENGTH. BUT GETAFIX ALSO HAS OTHER RECIPES UP HIS SLEEVE . . .

CACOFONIX, THE BARD. OPINION IS DIVIDED AS TO HIS MUSICAL GIFTS. CACOFONIX THINKS HE'S A GENIUS. EVERY-ONE ELSE THINKS HE'S UNSPEAKABLE. BUT SO LONG AS HE DOESN'T SPEAK, LET ALONE SING, EVERYBODY LIKES HIM . . .

FINALLY, VITALSTATISTIX, THE CHIEF OF THE TRIBE. MAJESTIC, BRAVE AND HOT-TEMPERED, THE OLD WARRIOR IS RESPECTED BY HIS MEN AND FEARED BY HIS ENEMIES. VITALSTATISTIX HIMSELF HAS ONLY ONE FEAR, HE IS AFRAID THE SKY MAY FALL ON HIS HEAD TOMORROW. BUT AS HE ALWAYS SAYS, TOMORROW NEVER COMES.

OH, WHAT A BEAUTIFUL MORNING OH, WHAT A BEAUTIFUL DAY... AND THE GAULS HAVE GOT A WONDERFUL FEELING EVERYTHING'S GOING THEIR WAY IN THEIR BRAND-NEW VILLAGE...

FOR AS YOU MAY REMEMBER..

THE ROMANS BURNED OUR VILLAGE TO THE GROUND*. CAESAR, ASHAMED OF WHAT THEY HAD DONE, TOLD HIS MEN TO REBUILD IT... FAIR ENOUGH, BUT THAT DOESN'T MEAN WE'RE ALL SQUARE. AND SO, DEAR FRIENDS...

* SEE ASTERIX AND SON

...I PROPOSE A TOAST TO THE REBIRTH OF THIS IMPOSING AND MAGNIFICENT SYMBOL OF OUR RESISTANCE TO THE ROMAN EMPIRE, AND IN PAYING SUITABLE TRIBUTE TO THIS, THE LAST BULWARK OF THE LIBERTIES OF OUR GREAT GAULISH NATION, I SAY TO YOU NOW...

I REALLY LIKED WATCHING THE ROMANS REBUILD OUR VILLAGE, ASTERIX!

YES, SPECIALLY WHEN THEY WERE GOING SLOW AND YOU THREW MENHIRS AT THEM TO SHOW YOU COULD STONEWALL TOO!

...I SAY TO YOU NOW...

WELL, THEY DID GET THE JOB DONE AHEAD OF SCHEDULE!

FEAR IS SOMETIMES A REMARKABLE STIMULUS, OBELIX!

HOW NICE TO HAVE BRAND-NEW HUTS TO LIVE IN!

YES, BUT I WOULDN'T HAVE MINDED A SPOT OF MODERN ARCHITECTURE WHILE THEY WERE ABOUT IT. FOR INSTANCE, VILLAS IN THE GALLO-ROMAN STYLE!

ROMAN COLUMNS ARE A TERRIBLE PRICE... SIMPLY RUINOUS!

THAT'S FUNNY... I DON'T SEEM TO SEE CACOFONIX THE BARD ANYWHERE!

SCRUNCH!

SCRUNCH!

WHY WERE YOU LOOKING FOR OUR VILLAGE IN PARTICULAR?

PAF!

TCHAC!

I COME FROM A DISTANT EASTERN COUNTRY, WHERE AN EX-LEGIONARY WHO IS NOW A MERCHANT TOLD ME ABOUT YOUR FAMOUS DEEDS. SO I'VE COME ALL THIS WAY TO ASK YOU FOR HELP? IT'S VERY IMPORTANT!

BUT BEFORE I TELL YOU ANY MORE, I'LL JUST RETRIEVE MY CARPET, IF I MAY.

PAF!

PIF!

LADIES, THAT CARPET IS MINE, AND I CAN PROVE IT.

THIS CARPET'S MINE, AND I'M NOT BUDGING!

IF YOU SAY SO!

? ?

(4A)

?

MUMMY!

?

HOW DID HE DO THAT, GETAFIX?

I'VE HEARD TELL OF THE STRANGE POWERS OF THESE FAKIRS BEFORE. THEY CAN CONCENTRATE HARD ENOUGH TO LEVITATE WHATEVER THEY LIKE.

(4B)

I COME FROM A KINGDOM WHICH LIES IN THE VALLEY OF THE GANGES. OUR CLIMATE IS HOT AND DRY, EXCEPT FOR A FEW MONTHS EVERY YEAR WHEN THE RAINS FALL, WATERING OUR CROPS. THAT IS THE MONSOON SEASON.

I HOPE HE HASN'T COME ALL THIS WAY JUST TO TALK ABOUT THE WEATHER!

BUT WE MUST HAVE OFFENDED THE GOD INDRA*, BECAUSE THE MONSOON SEASON WILL SOON BE OVER, AND WE HAVEN'T HAD A DROP OF RAIN YET. THE DRY SEASON WILL BE BACK, BRINGING WITH IT FAMINE AND HARD-SHIP FOR OUR PEOPLE.

*GOD OF THE WATERS

OUR GOOD KING, RAJAH WATZIT, HAS A DAUGHTER, THE SWEET AND LOVELY PRINCESS ORINJADE...

AND THE GURU* WHO SPEAKS WITH THE GODS, HOODUNNIT, DECREED THAT IF NO RAIN FELL BEFORE THE END OF THE MONSOON, IN A THOUSAND AND ONE HOURS' TIME, PRINCESS ORINJADE MUST BE SACRIFICED TO APPEASE THE WRATH OF THE GODS!

TEE HEE HEE!

* LEADER OF A RELIGIOUS SECT

BUT IF EVEN YOUR RAJAH DOESN'T HOLD THE RAINS OF POWER, I DON'T QUITE SEE HOW WE CAN HELP YOU!

I THINK I DO, THOUGH. I FANCY OUR VISITOR WANTS TO BORROW THE BARD. HIS SINGING WILL BRING RAIN EVEN IN AN INDIAN SUMMER.

OH, YES... I WAS FORGETTING CACOFONIX HAS A NEW STRING TO HIS LYRE THESE DAYS!

ALL RIGHT, FAKIR! WE'LL LEND YOU OUR BARD, AND ASTERIX AND OBELIX WILL GO WITH YOU TOO.

HOW DARE YOU SAY I MAKE IT RAIN? IT'S NOT TRUE! LISTEN TO THIS!

THE RAIN IN GAUL...

...FALLS MAINLY DOWN THE WALL...

HEY! IT'S RAINING DOWN THE INSIDE OF THE WALL!

12

PHEW! I THOUGHT I'D NEVER SEE YOU AGAIN!

YOU KNOW WE'D NEVER LET YOU DOWN... OH, SORRY!

HUH! PACHYDERM! PACHYDERM YOURSELF!

I'M HUNGRY!

I CAN SEE A LITTLE CHEF DOWN THERE!

TRY OUR ROAST BOAR, AND THEN YOU WON'T EVEN MIND IF THE SKY DOES FALL ON YOUR HEADS!

RESTAVR

AND THE SAME AGAIN FOR US, PLEASE, CHEF!

!?

RESTA

THESE SELF-SERVICE PLACES ARE A GOOD NOTION!

WOULD YOU LIKE A SLICE OF BOAR, WATZIZNEHM?

I'M AN ASCETIC. ASCETICS NEVER EAT MEAT.

SCRUNCH!

SCRUNCH!

OVER THREE WEEKS, AND HE STILL ISN'T EATING. IF YOU ASK ME, ASTERIX, HE'S NOT NORMAL!

AH, A ROMAN CAMP! I'LL JUST MAKE SURE WE'RE FLYING THE RIGHT WAY.

HEY, IS THIS THE WAY TO ROME?

HIC!

YUP... HIC!... ANYWAY... HAEC!... ALL ROADS... HOC!... LEAD TO ROME!

THANKS!

!

WELL, INCAUTIUS, GAULISH WINE TOO MUCH FOR YOU, EH?

TOO TRUE! I SWEAR I'LL NEVER BE I* OVER THE VIII* AGAIN!

*ONE *EIGHT

13

IT WILL SOON BE DARK. WHERE ARE WE GOING TO STOP OVER TONIGHT, WATZIZNEHM?

THERE'S NO TIME TO STOP! YOU CAN SLEEP ON THE CARPET. IT'S VERY COMFORTABLE.

AREN'T YOU GOING TO SLEEP?

I'M USED TO STAYING AWAKE ALL NIGHT. ANYWAY, I CAN ONLY SLEEP ON A BED OF NAILS!

TAP!
TAP!
TAP!

MEANWHILE, FAR AWAY...

DEAR ORINJADE, IF THE FAITHFUL WATZIZNEHM DOESN'T ARRIVE IN TIME, WITH THE ANSWER TO ALL OUR PROBLEMS, THE INFAMOUS HOODUNNIT WILL CARRY OUT HIS THREAT. THE PEOPLE, FEARING FAMINE, WILL SUPPORT HIM!

I TRUST WATZIZNEHM, FATHER! HE WILL RETURN WITH THE GAULISH MIRACLE-WORKER BEFORE THE THOUSAND AND ONE HOURS ARE UP!

MEANWHILE, HALF OF THOSE THOUSAND AND ONE HOURS IS UP ALREADY, AND IT STILL ISN'T RAINING, O DIVINE PRINCESS!

WRETCH! WE KNOW THAT THE SOLE AIM OF YOUR EVIL PLOTS IS TO BECOME RULER OF THIS KINGDOM ONCE YOU HAVE DISPOSED OF THE ONLY TRUE HEIR TO THE THRONE! BUT YOU HAVEN'T DONE IT YET, HOODUNNIT!

YOUR GRIEF DELUDES YOU, GREAT RAJAH! THE GOD INDRA HIMSELF TOLD ME HIS WILL!

SEE THAT CLOUDLESS SKY, AND THE PITILESS SUN BEATING DOWN ON YOUR WHOLE KINGDOM? ISN'T THAT A SIGN THAT THE GODS THINK YOU'RE A HAS-BEEN, WATZIT?

THE GODS ARE NOT AS CRUEL AS YOU SAY. THEY WILL GUIDE THE SAVIOURS OF THE PEOPLE SAFELY TO US. THEY MUST BE ON THEIR WAY NOW!

JUST AT THE MOMENT, THE SAVIOURS OF THE PEOPLE ARE PREPARING FOR THEIR FIRST NIGHT IN THE AIR.

ASTERIX, WHAT'S A PACHYDERM?

SHUT UP AND GO TO SLEEP, OBELIX!

SOON AFTERWARDS...

ZZZZZ! ZZZZZZ! ZZZZZZ!

16

AFTER NINETY-SIX HOURS' FLYING TIME...

WE ARE NOW APPROACHING **ROME**

I'LL COME DOWN SO THAT WE CAN GET A CLOSER VIEW OF THIS GREAT AND MAGNIFICENT CITY!

GREAT? HUH! IT'S NOT THAT MUCH BIGGER THAN OUR VILLAGE!

THAT FEVER HAS LEFT ME VERY WEAK!

AESCULAPIUS WAS WATCHING OVER YOU, O CAESAR. JUST A CASE OF GRAVEDO ASIATICA*.

* ASIAN FLU

COME OUT ON THE TERRACE AND BREATHE THE FRESH AIR WAFTING OVER ROME, AND YOU'LL FEEL BETTER!

IN MY FEVERED DELIRIUM, I KEPT SEEING THOSE INDOMITABLE GAULS FROM ARMORICA. ALL OVER THE PLACE! IT WAS LIKE A NIGHTMARE!

WELL, I NEVER! HI, JULIUS, OLD CHAP!

?!

CAESAR AND HIS DOCTOR HAVE GONE TO BED. IN THEIR FEVERED DELIRIUM, THEY KEEP SAYING THEY SAW INDOMITABLE GAULS AND AN ASIAN FAKIR!

AND THE GAULS AND THE ASIAN FLEW!

*GOD OF WINE

SPLOSH!

A SHIP! I THINK THEY'VE SEEN US!

WELCOME ABOARD. I'M ONTHEPREMISES, A GREEK MERCHANT!

I'M ASTERIX THE GAUL. YOU HAVEN'T SEEN ANY FAKIRS FALLING, HAVE YOU?

NO, IT'S BEEN RAINING CATS AND DOGS, WHICH THE ORACLE METOFFIS AS USUAL FAILED TO FORECAST, BUT NO FAKIRS.

THEN HE'S LOST AT SEA! WE'RE DONE FOR!

...WHILE THE RAGING SEAS DID ROAR, AND THE STORMY WINDS DID BLOW... HIC!

...AND WE JOLLY FAKIR-BOYS WERE ALL UP... HIC! ALOFT...

THAT'S WATZIZNEHM'S VOICE!

WHATS HIS NAME... WATZIZNEHM?

...AND THE LANDLUBBERS LYING DOWN BELOW... HIC!

WHAT HAVE YOU GOT IN THOSE JARS?

CAN'T YOU TELL? WINE, IF THERE'S ANY LEFT.

IS THIS BY ANY CHANCE YOUR FAKIR?

...BELOW BELOW...

BY TOUTATIS, HE'S GOT A FEW JARS INSIDE HIM!

SO MUCH FOR THE ASCETIC LIFE! AS A FAKIR HE'S A FAKER!

AND **HE** CALLS HIMSELF A POET!

19

GOOD THING WE WERE NEAR THE COAST!

OH, WOULDN'T THIS MAKE THE PIRATES LAUGH!

TO THINK OF THE SONG AND DANCE ODYSSEUS MADE ABOUT THE SIRENS!

...AND WE JOLLY FAKIR-BOYS WERE ALL... HIC!

I KNEW I COULD WAKE HIM UP!

YES, BUT HE'S NOT IN GREAT SHAPE. HARDLY SURPRISING AFTER SUCH A LONG FAST!

SAME AS ME! I FEEL A BIT WEAK AND FEEBLE TOO!

AND WHAT ARE YOU GOING TO DO ABOUT MY SHIP?

WEAK AND FEEBLE AS HE MAY BE, OBELIX IS GOING TO HELP ME RE-FLOAT IT, ONTHEPREMISES!

OH, SO I'M NOT EVEN ALLOWED A MOMENT'S WEAKNESS, RIGHT?

SHUT UP AND PUSH, OBELIX!

WHEN I TELL ODYSSEUS MY OWN ODYSSEY, HE'LL NEVER BELIEVE ME!

...HIC!...
LYING DOWN BELOW!

TUT, TUT!

WELL, I'LL BE GLAD TO BE BACK ON THE COMFORT OF THE FLYING CARPET!

YES... WHERE IS IT?

THE CARPET!! WE'VE LOST THE CARPET!!!

21

MEANWHILE, VERY FAR AWAY...

LEMUHNADE, MY FAITHFUL LEMUHNADE, DO YOU SEE ANYONE COMING?

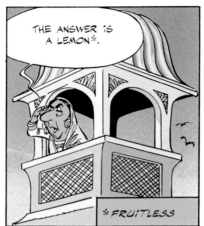

THE ANSWER IS A LEMON*.

*FRUITLESS

WELL, OWZAT, MY WICKED HENCH-MAN, THE HEIR OF THIS KINGDOM WILL SOON BREATHE HER LAST OF THE AIR OF THIS KINGDOM! RATHER DRY, EH? HERE'S TO THE SUCCESS OF OUR PLANS!

YOU ALWAYS DID HAVE A DRY WIT, O DIVINE MASTER. CHEERS! AND MAY THE FORCES OF EVIL MAKE THAT TALKATIVE FOOL WATZIZNEHM DRY UP FOR EVER!

I'M A FOOL, AND I'VE GOT A TERRIBLE THIRST!

WELL, I'M NO FOOL, BUT I'VE GOT A TERRIBLE HUNGER!

WHY BLAME YOURSELF? IT'S NOT YOUR FAULT!

I HAVE COMMITTED THE SIN OF GLUTTONY! NET RESULT: A SPLITTING HEAD-ACHE AND A FRIGHTFUL WASTE OF TIME!

WELL, WE'LL SOON BE FLYING OVER ATHENS, AND THEN WE LEAVE GREECE BEHIND!

19A

SURE ENOUGH, AFTER A HUNDRED AND FIFTY HOURS' FLYING TIME...

REMEMBER OUR TRIP TO THE OLYMPIC GAMES, OBELIX?

YES, SPECIALLY THERMOS'S LITTLE RESTAURANT AND HIS STUFFED VINE LEAVES, KEBABS, OLIVES, WATER MELON AND RESINATED WINE!*
(SIGH)

* SEE ASTERIX AT THE OLYMPIC GAMES.

19B

THE HOURS PASS INEXORABLY BY... THEREBY HANGS MANY A TALE.

WE SHALL SOON BE LEAVING THE SEA FOR THE LAST TIME AND FLYING OVER THE LANDS OF THE ORIENT!

GOOD! WE CAN COME DOWN AND HAVE SOME DINNER AT LAST!

TWANG!

OOOWWW!!

?

OBELIX!

YOWL! YOWL! YOWL!

QUICK! HE'S FALLING!!!

I CAN STILL SEE HIM... I'LL TRY FLYING UNDERNEATH HIM!

20A

POF!

ALL RIGHT, OBELIX?

WHAT HAPPENED TO ME? WHAT HAPPENED TO ME?

WOOF! WOOF!

THEY'RE STILL SHOOTING AT US, BY TOUTATIS!

WE'RE OVER TYRE*. YES, IT IS RATHER TIRESOME.

* PHOENICIAN PORT. SEE ASTERIX AND THE BLACK GOLD

LET'S GET SHOT OF THIS LOT QUICK!!!

I DON'T LIKE IT A BIT!

OH, YOU SOON GET USED TO IT.

20B

24

THE SKY OVER RAJAH WATZIT'S KINGDOM IS STILL RELENTLESSLY CLEAR, AND WE ARE NOW ONLY THREE HUNDRED HOURS FROM ZERO HOUR, THE TIME SET FOR THE SACRIFICE OF PRINCESS ORINJADE.

LEMUHNADE, LEMUHNADE, DO YOU SEE ANYONE COMING?

THE ANSWER'S STILL A LEMON...

YOUR WEATHER FORECASTS HAVE BEEN ACCURATE SO FAR, OWZAT! NOT A CLOUD ON THE HORIZON. BUT SUPPOSE WATZIZ-NEHM BRINGS THAT GAUL BACK IN TIME TO MAKE IT RAIN?

I DON'T BELIEVE IN THAT KIND OF MIRACLE, O DIVINE MASTER. FLYING CARPETS ARE ONE THING, BUT RAIN-MAKING IS SHEER SCIENCE FICTION!

I'M HUNGRY!

SIGH!

FOR YOUR INFORMATION, WE ARE NOW FLYING OVER PERSIA, AND TELL YOUR FRIEND HE MUST LIVE ON HIS HUMP A LITTLE LONGER. WE'VE NO TIME TO WASTE!

EATING IS NEVER A WASTE OF TIME! ARE YOU SURPRISED I'VE GOT THE HUMP?

?

LOOK, IT'S NOTHING WHAT-EVER TO DO WITH ME!!!

CRASH

WATCH OUT! THE CARPET'S ON FIRE!

THE CARPET'S BEEN HOLED! I CAN'T HOLD IT STEADY!

SPLOSH!

WHAT LUCK I MANAGED TO DIVERT OUR FLIGHT PATH TOWARDS THIS RIVER!

YES, BUT NOW WE'RE ALL WASHED UP!

THIS POURS COLD WATER ON OUR PLANS!

AND THE FLYING CARPET'S MORE OF A BATH MAT NOW.

THAT'S TORN IT! WE CAN'T GO ON. I SHOULD HAVE BROUGHT A SPARE CARPET ALONG.

MAYBE WE CAN GET IT MENDED?

THAT'S POSSIBLE... IN FACT, WE MAY HAVE FALLEN ON OUR FEET, LANDING HERE! PERSIA IS FAMOUS FOR ITS CARPETS. IF WE GO ON ALONG THIS RIVER, WE MIGHT FIND A CARPET MENDER.

BUT AFTER A WALK OF SEVERAL HOURS...

WE'VE HAD THE RUG PULLED OUT FROM UNDER US!

I'M HUNGRY!

AND TIME IS PASSING. WE'RE DONE FOR NOW.

LOOK... A VILLAGE, OVER THERE!

22A

HELLO. I SEE YOU HAVE SOME VERY FINE CARPETS!

I'M A CARPET MAKER. I'M WASHING THE ONE I'VE JUST FINISHED WEAVING.

IF YOU WANT A WELL WASHED CARPET, I'VE GOT ONE!

COULD YOU MEND THIS?

SORRY, CAN'T BE DONE!

WHY NOT?

BECAUSE I ONLY MEND THE CARPETS I MAKE AND SELL MYSELF! WHAT'S MORE NOBODY AROUND HERE WOULD AGREE TO MEND A CARPET THAT WASN'T MADE IN PERSIA!

?

22B

26

LEMUHNADE, LEMUHNADE, DO YOU SEE ANYONE COMING?

THE ANSWER'S STILL A LEM...

OH, FORGET IT!

TEEHEE! IF THE CLEPSYDRA* IS KEEPING GOOD TIME, WE'RE ONLY A HUNDRED AND EIGHTY HOURS FROM ZERO HOUR!

WHEN YOU CAN ZERO IN ON THE THRONE, O DIVINE MASTER... TEEHEE!

* ANCIENT WATER CLOCK.

MEANWHILE...

OH, SO YOU CAN'T MEND FOREIGN HOLES, IS THAT IT?

FOR A START, WE'RE NOT FOREIGNERS, WE'RE GAULS!

YES, YES, OF COURSE! BUT I REALLY CAN'T MEND YOUR CARPET. I DON'T HAVE THE NECESSARY SPARE PART.

HOW MUCH WOULD ONE OF YOUR OWN CARPETS COST?

TO YOU, ONLY ONE SILVER TALENT*!

* CURRENCY OF THE ANCIENT PERSIANS.

ONE SILVER TALENT DOESN'T SEEM VERY MUCH FOR A CARPET!

PERSIAN TALENTS WEIGH THIRTY KILOS EACH. YOU NEED A TALENT FOR MAKING MONEY TO GET ONE!

TAP! TAP! TAP!

THESE PERSIANS ARE CRAZY!

OUR CARPET'S IN HOLES, AND WE DON'T HAVE ANY TALENT FOR GETTING ANOTHER. **ALL IS LOST!**

OH, I DON'T KNOW. WE COULD HELP OURSELVES TO ONE.

OBELIX IS RIGHT! NO USE BEING HOLIER THAN THOU IN A HOLE LIKE THIS.

NO! WE CAN'T STEAL AWAY ON A STOLEN CARPET!

WELL, I'LL JUST GO ON BRUSHING MY CARPETS.

THE SCYTHIANS*!!! THE SCYTHIAN PIRATES ARE COMING!!!

* PEOPLE ORIGINATING FROM THE CRIMEA.

THE PIRATES WILL STEAL OUR CARPETS AND BURN OUR HOUSES DOWN AGAIN!!!

I BEG YOU! IF YOU HAVE ANY POWERS, HELP US TO MEND MATTERS, OR IT WILL BE THE END OF OUR VILLAGE!!!

SORRY, CAN'T BE DONE!

WHY NOT?

BECAUSE YOUR PROBLEMS ARE FOREIGN TO US, AND WE DON'T HAVE THE NECESSARY SPARE PART EITHER!

WHAT'S THAT?

A CARPET!

TAKE THIS ONE, BY AHURA MAZDA*!

DONE, BY TOUTATIS!

SLAP

*GOD OF THE ANCIENT PERSIANS.

CACOFONIX, YOU WAIT HERE WITH DOGMATIX. THIS WON'T TAKE LONG!

A BIT OF ACTION AT LAST!

WATZIZNEHM, CAN YOU FLY THROUGH THE RANKS OF THE SCYTHIANS QUITE LOW?

PLANNING TO SCYTHE THROUGH THEM?

CRASH!
BANG!
WALLOP!

BY THE GREAT GODDESS*! WE MUST FLY FROM THESE DEMONS OF THE SKY!

* PRINCIPAL DEITY OF THE SCYTHIANS.

OVER ALREADY? I PREFER ROMANS. THEY LAST LONGER!

LONG LIVE OUR HEROES!

LONG LIVE OUR RESCUERS!

AND THEY DID IT WITH **MY** CARPET, TOO!

WOOF! WOOF! WOOF!

WE OWE YOU A LOT! WHAT CAN WE GIVE YOU, BESIDES THE CARPET?

SOMETHING TO EAT!

AND SO A LITTLE LATER...

THESE LITTLE GREY THINGS ARE VERY NICE!

ONLY POOR MAN'S FARE! FISH EGGS... WE CALL THEM KHAVIAR! THEY'RE VERY NOURISHING, THOUGH!

ONE EGG WILL DO FOR ME, THEN!

WHAT'S THAT?

ROAST CAMEL! AS GOOD AS DROMEDARY, BUT A BETTER BUY, BECAUSE IT HAS TWO HUMPS!

SCRUNCH! SCRUNCH!

A ROAST CAMEL MAY BE A GOOD BUY, BUT IT'S NOT UP TO A GOOD ROAST BOAR!

NO ONE WOULD EVER KNOW, SEEING THE AMOUNT YOU ATE!

RIGHT... NOW WE'VE FILLED UP AGAIN, WE MUST MAKE UP FOR LOST TIME AND FLY STRAIGHT TO RAJAH WATZIT'S KINGDOM!

I WILL NOT SEE YOU DIE, DEAR ORINJADE! I'D RATHER ABDICATE IN FAVOUR OF HOODUNNIT.

DON'T WORRY, FATHER! WATZIZNEHM ISN'T JUST ANYONE!

NO KNIGHTS IN SHINING ARMOUR RIDING TO WATZIT'S AID AS THE THOUSAND AND ONE HOURS TICK BY, OWZAT!

NO, IT WOULD TAKE A THOUSAND AND ONE NIGHTS TO SAVE HIM AND THE PRINCESS NOW!

O HOODUNNIT, DIVINE MASTER, SUPPOSE THERE'S STILL NO RAIN WHEN YOU'VE EXECUTED THE PRINCESS?

INDRA WILL CALL FOR MORE ROYAL BLOOD... AND IT'LL BE OFF WITH THE RAJAH'S HEAD!

BUT SUPPOSE IT STILL DOESN'T RAIN?

IT WON'T MATTER A BIT, BECAUSE BY THEN I'LL BE RAJAH MYSELF. HO, HO, HO!

HOWEVER, THE VALIANT PERSIAN CARPET FLIES TIRELESSLY ON, WHETHER CROSSING BAKING DESERTS...

...OR FACING THE BITTER WEATHER OF THE MOUNTAIN PEAKS.

AS SCENERY GOES, THIS LEAVES ME COLD!

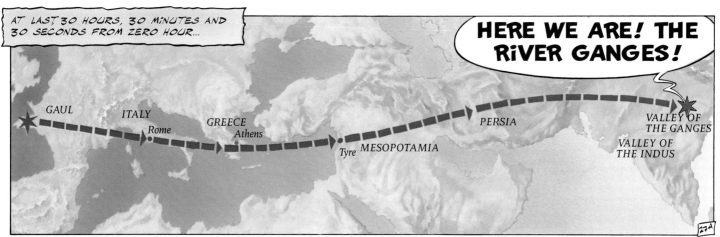

AT LAST, 30 HOURS, 30 MINUTES AND 30 SECONDS FROM ZERO HOUR...

HERE WE ARE! THE RIVER GANGES!

GAUL

ITALY
Rome

GREECE
Athens

Tyre MESOPOTAMIA

PERSIA

VALLEY OF THE GANGES

VALLEY OF THE INDUS

LOOKS A BIT GUNGY, AS RIVERS GO!

WHAT ARE ALL THOSE PEOPLE DOING, SQUELCHING ABOUT IN THE MUD?

THE GANGES IS A SACRED RIVER. EVEN IN THIS DROUGHT, THE PEOPLE STILL COME HERE TO WASH, THUS PURIFYING THEIR SOULS AND BODIES. SEE?

CLEAR AS MUD! THESE INDIANS ARE CRAZY!

TAP!
TAP!
TAP!

AND HERE IS RAJAH WATZIT'S PALACE!

I SEE WATZIZNEHM'S CARPET COMING IN ... HE'S ABOUT TO BRAKE...

HE'S GOT THE GAULS ON BOARD!!! IS THIS OUR LUCKY BREAK?

CURSES!

31

THERE, FATHER, WASN'T I RIGHT TO TRUST THE FAITHFUL WATZIZNEHM?

OUCH! I SHOULD HAVE WATCHED MY STEP!

AS PROMISED, GREAT RAJAH, I BRING YOU THE GAULS WHO CAN MAKE IT RAIN!

MAY THE THIRTY MILLION VEDIC GODS CARRY THEM TO NIRVANA * FOR THE MIRACLE THEY ARE ABOUT TO WORK!

* INDIAN PARADISE.

OUR BARD'S THE ONE WHO CAN MAKE IT RAIN WHEN HE SINGS!

WOW!

THE 1001 HOURS ARE RUNNING OUT, AND OUR NUMBER WILL SOON BE UP, BUT WOULD YOU LIKE SOME REFRESHMENTS BEFORE YOU TRY WORKING YOUR MIRACLE?

TEE HEE!

A MIRACULOUSLY REFRESHING IDEA!

THE GAULISH MIRACLE-WORKER WILL MAKE IT RAIN THIS AFTERNOON. ALL THE RAJAH'S SUBJECTS ARE SUMMONED TO THE PALACE TO WITNESS THE MIRACLE.

MAKING HEAVY WEATHER OF IT AS USUAL! THEY'RE ALWAYS PROMISING RAIN, AND IT ALWAYS TURNS OUT FINE!

OH, FOR A PATCH OF GREY SKY AGAIN! OH, TO WASH IN RAIN, NOT MUD!

IF WATZIZNEHM IS RIGHT, THOSE GAULS WILL PUT A DAMPER ON OUR PLANS!

HERE IS THE GAUL WHO WILL INVOKE THE GODS IN SONG, TO PERSUADE THEM TO SEND RAIN FROM HEAVEN TO WATER OUR CROPS!

ARE YOU SURE THIS IS GOING TO WORK?

QUITE SURE. I'M AFRAID IT ALWAYS DOES.

OLING! DING! DONG!

YOU NEVER HAD AN AUDIENCE LIKE THIS BEFORE, CACOFONIX! PLAY UP!

...

?

...

WHY ARE YOU PLAYING UP NOW?

OH NO... DON'T SAY YOU'VE LOST YOUR VOICE!!

I ASK YOU! WHEN WE DON'T WANT HIM TO SING, HE SINGS, AND WHEN WE DO WANT HIM TO SING, HE CAN'T! NOW WE'LL REALLY HAVE TO FACE THE MUSIC!

BY ALL THE AVATARS*! THOSE GAULS WILL HAVE TO CHANGE THIER TUNE!

HO, HO, HO!

* INCARNATIONS AND METAMORPHOSES OF THE INDIAN GODS.

A LITTLE LATER...

WE'D BETTER GO TO HOWDOO'S ON FOOT, SO AS NOT TO AROUSE THE EVIL HOODUNNIT'S SUSPICIONS!

?

I SAY... THOSE COWS...

I KNOW WHAT YOU'RE GOING TO ASK! COWS ARE SACRED HERE. THEY'RE FREE TO GO WHERE THEY LIKE, AND NO ONE MAY HARM THEM. ANYWAY, WE DON'T CARE MUCH FOR MEAT HERE!

I ONLY HOPE WILD BOAR AREN'T SACRED HERE TOO!

HERE WE ARE! HOW DO, HOWDOO?

! ! !

31A

SAME TO YOU, WATZIZNEHM! YOU'RE WELCOME TOO, NOBLE STRANGERS!

HOWDOO, MEET MY GAULISH FRIENDS, WHO URGENTLY NEED YOUR HELP.

HOWDOO IS THE BEST ELEPHANT TRAINER AROUND. HE GETS HIS BEASTS TO PERFORM AMAZING FEATS!

A HANDY FEAT, BUT WHAT'S SO AMAZING ABOUT IT?

CRACK!

IT'S EASY TO PICK UP!

CRAACK!

!

OH, SORRY, DOGMATIX. I FORGOT YOU HATE TO SEE ANYONE PICK THE PRETTY TREES!

HOOOWL

31B

YOU ASKED ME WHAT A PACHYDERM WAS, OBELIX. THAT IS!

?!

HUH! NOT MUCH LIKE ME, IS IT?

SNIFF!

YOU'RE VERY WELL TRAINED, STRANGER! I CAN GIVE YOU A JOB IF YOU LIKE!

?

THAT'S NOT WHAT WE'RE HERE FOR, HOWDOO. THE GAULISH BARD HAS LOST HIS VOICE AND CAN'T SING. THE DOCTORS HAVE PRESCRIBED A BATH OF ELEPHANT'S MILK MIXED WITH ELEPHANT DUNG AND ELEPHANT HAIR!

BOTHER THAT! I KNOW A MUCH QUICKER CURE! I HAD AN ELEPHANT WHO COULDN'T TRUMPET BECAUSE HIS TRUNK WAS STUFFED UP. I ONLY HAD TO BLOW DOWN IT VERY HARD!

32A

SINCE WHEN HE'S TENDED TO GET WIND, BUT HE CAN BLOW HIS OWN TRUMPET NOW!

...

I CAN DO THE SAME FOR HIM IF YOU LIKE?

NO, THANKS... I THINK HE'D PREFER THE FIRST PRESCRIPTION!

WHAT A SHAME... IT WOULD HAVE BEEN EASY WITH A NOSE LIKE THAT!

LATER...

WE'LL LEAVE YOU NOW, CACOFONIX, BUT WE'LL BE BACK TOMORROW MORNING!

WHEN YOU'RE READY TO WORK MIRACLES AGAIN!

TEEHEE!

TEEHEE!

THE GAULISH BARD IS AT HOWDOO'S. HE'LL BE ON HIS OWN TONIGHT!

EXCELLENT! NOW THIS IS WHAT YOU HAVE TO DO...

32B

WHEN NIGHT HAS FALLEN, EIGHTEEN HOURS FROM ZERO HOUR...

WHAT A PONG! IT MAKES ME GAG!

WELL, WE NEEDN'T WASTE TIME GAGGING **HIM** SINCE HE CAN'T SPEAK.

I CAN STAND MOST THINGS... THE NIGHT, THE JUNGLE BY NIGHT, BUT THIS STINK IS TOO MUCH FOR ME!

THE SOONER WE GET THERE, THE BETTER FOR US!

BY NOW OUR MEN WILL BE TAKING THE GAUL TO THE SACRED SANCTUARY OF THE ELEPHANTS' GRAVE-YARD, IN THE HEART OF THE JUNGLE!

TEEHEEHEE! WHEN HE'S FOUND, THE FURIOUS ELEPHANTS WILL HAVE TRAMPLED HIM TO THE THICKNESS OF A DRACHMA*!

* GREEK COIN USED IN INDIA.

NEXT MORNING, WITH TEN HOURS TO GO TO ZERO HOUR...

TIME TO GO AND GET CACOFONIX! IT'LL BE QUICKER BY CARPET!

WHAT ABOUT MY BREAKFAST?

THERE'S A TIME AND A PLACE FOR EVERYTHING!

33A

I CAN'T WAIT TO SEE IF THE CURE HAS WORKED!

I CAN'T WAIT TO KNOW WHEN IT'LL BE THE TIME AND THE PLACE FOR MY BREAKFAST. I FEEL SO FLAT WHEN MY TUMMY'S EMPTY!

AND YOUR TUMMY'S NOT THE ONLY EMPTY PART YOU!

THERE, YOU ADMIT IT YOURSELF!

THEY'RE OFF TO FETCH THE BARD! TRY TO DELAY THEM OWZAT!

THAT'S EASY... MY CARPET'S PARKED QUITE CLOSE!

NOW FOR THE SHOWDOWN, WATZIZNEHM!

33B

TANTAN AAARAT

TRUMPETING NICELY NOW, ISN'T HE?

THE ELEPHANTS ARE MOVING ASIDE!

THANK TOUTATIS HE'S SAFE AND SOUND!!!

THANKS TO THE SMELL CLINGING TO HIM, THE ELEPHANTS THOUGHT HE WAS ONE OF THEM! WHAT LUCK FOR HIM!

I KNEW I HAD NOTHING IN COMMON WITH THOSE PACHYDERMS!

YOU'VE STILL LOST YOUR VOICE, BUT YOU'RE ALIVE, THAT'S THE MAIN THING!

TANTANTARAAAA!

39A

BUT WE ARE NOW ONLY TWO HOURS FROM ZERO HOUR, AND PREPARATIONS FOR THE SACRIFICE ARE ALREADY UNDER WAY.

I SHALL DISPOSE OF THE DAUGHTER FIRST, THEN THE FATHER, AND THEN, LIKE MY COUSIN IZNOGOUD, I SHALL BE RAJAH INSTEAD OF THE RAJAH!

WHAT CAN THE GAULS BE DOING? WHERE IS WATZIZNEHM?

WATZIZNEHM IS STILL BUSY WITH HIS SUMMIT MEETING. WHICH OF THE TWO FAKIRS WILL WIN? WATZIZNEHM? OWZAT? IT'S ALL STILL IN THE AIR...

SKAMBHA* BRING THE SKY DOWN ON YOUR HEAD!!

PUSHAN** TURN YOU INTO AN OLD GOAT!

* COSMIC PILLAR GOD HOLDING UP THE SKY.   ** GOD OF DOMESTIC ANIMALS.

39B

43

At five minutes to zero hour...

Better resign yourself, Princess! Still no rain! Your last hour has come!

May Vishnu* strangle you, evil guru!

* GOD WITH MANY ARMS.

May my sacrifice persuade heaven to shower its blessings on you once again! If it does not, beware of those serpents who are tricking you for their own evil ends!

LONG LIVE OUR PRINCESS WHO IS ABOUT TO DIE FOR US!!!

POOR SILLY IDIOTS!

FIVE... FOUR... THREE...

TWO... ONE...

ZERO!

TCHAC!

46

FOR THE RAIN IT ♪ ♪ RAINETH EVERY DAY...

DON'T BE SO WET!!!

THE GAULISH MIRACLE!

43A

AND THE GAULISH MIRACLE HAS BROUGHT THE MONSOON ON AT LAST. THE CROPS ARE SAVED, THE WATERS OF THE GANGES HAVE RISEN AGAIN, AND ALL THE INDIANS ARE HAPPY...

...WITH A FEW EXCEPTIONS!

SHEER SCIENCE FICTION, THAT IDIOT SAID!

GOING TO BE RAJAH INSTEAD OF THE RAJAH, THAT CROOK SAID!

YOU HAVE GIVEN US SO MUCH! WHAT CAN WE EVER GIVE YOU IN RETURN?

SOMETHING TO EAT!!!

?!

43B

THE END —UDERZO · 6·87